What a Mess!

by Damian Harvey and Charlie Alder

Dad had a tin of paint
and a brush.

Mum had a ladder
and a roller.

"What are you doing?"
said Jazz.

Mum was painting the wall.

"Can I help?" said Jazz.

"Don't make a mess,"
said Mum.

Jazz painted the wall.

"Look at me," she said.

"Well done," said Mum.

"You did not make a mess."

Dad was painting the door.

"Can I help?" said Jazz.

"Don't make a mess,"
said Dad.

"Look!" said Jazz.

"Look at me.

I am painting the door."

"Well done," said Dad.

"You did not make a mess."

15

"Oh no!" said Mum.

"Oh no!" said Dad.

"Oh no!" said Jazz.
"What a mess!"

Story trail

Start

Start at the beginning of the story trail. Ask your child to retell the story in their own words, pointing to each picture in turn to recall the sequence of events.

Independent Reading

This series is designed to provide an opportunity for your child to read on their own. These notes are written for you to help your child choose a book and to read it independently.

In school, your child's teacher will often be using reading books which have been banded to support the process of learning to read.

Use the book band colour your child is reading in school to help you make a good choice. *What a Mess!* is a good choice for children reading at Yellow Band in their classroom to read independently.

The aim of independent reading is to read this book with ease, so that your child enjoys the story and relates it to their own experiences.

About the book

Mum and Dad are decorating the house. Jazz wants to help and they are happy to let her, as long as she does not make a mess. Jazz makes no mess at all, unlike her pet dog ...

Before reading

Help your child to learn how to make good choices by asking: "Why did you choose this book? Why do you think you will enjoy it?" Look at the cover together and ask: "What do you think the story will be about?" Support your child to think of what they already know about the story context. Read the title aloud and ask: "What do you think they are going to be doing in the story? Do you think something might go wrong? Why do you think that?" Remind your child that they can try to sound out the letters to make a word if they get stuck. Decide together whether your child will read the story independently or read it aloud to you. When books are short, as at Yellow Band, your child may wish to do both!

During reading

If reading aloud, support your child if they hesitate or ask for help by telling the word. Remind your child of what they know and what they can do independently. If reading to themselves, remind your child that they can come and ask for your help if stuck.

After reading

Support comprehension by asking your child to tell you about the story. Use the story trail to encourage your child to retell the story in the right sequence, in their own words.

Give your child a chance to respond to the story: "Did you have a favourite part? Do you have a pet who makes a mess sometimes?"

Help your child think about the messages in the book that go beyond the story and ask: "Do you think Jazz's dog will be in trouble? Why / why not?"

Extending learning

Help your child understand the story structure by using the same sentence patterns and adding some new elements. "Let's make up a new story about Jazz helping her parents in the garden.

Mum was watering the flowers. 'Can I help?' asked Jazz.

'Yes,' said Mum. 'But do not make a mess.'

Jazz watered the flowers.

Now you try. What will Jazz be helping with in your story?"

Your child's teacher will be talking about punctuation at Yellow Band. On a few of the pages, check your child can recognise capital letters, question marks, exclamation marks and full stops by asking them to point these out.

Franklin Watts
First published in Great Britain in 2019
by The Watts Publishing Group

Series Editors: Jackie Hamley and Melanie Palmer
Series Advisors: Dr Sue Bodman and Glen Franklin
Series Designer: Peter Scoulding

A CIP catalogue record for this book is
available from the British Library.

ISBN 978 1 4451 6792 3 (hbk)
ISBN 978 1 4451 6794 7 (pbk)
ISBN 978 1 4451 6793 0 (library ebook)

Printed in China

Franklin Watts
An imprint of
Hachette Children's Group
Part of The Watts Publishing Group
Carmelite House
50 Victoria Embankment
London EC4Y 0DZ

An Hachette UK Company
www.hachette.co.uk

www.franklinwatts.co.uk

FSC
www.fsc.org
MIX
Paper from
responsible sources
FSC® C104740